ARCHITECTS MAKE ZIGZAGS

Looking at Architecture from A to Z

Drawings by Roxie Munro
Text by Diane Maddex

THE PRESERVATION PRESS

The Preservation Press
National Trust for Historic Preservation
1785 Massachusetts Avenue, N.W.
Washington, D.C. 20036

The National Trust for Historic Preservation is the only private, nonprofit national organization chartered by Congress (in 1949) to encourage public participation in the preservation of sites, buildings and objects significant in American history and culture. Support is provided by membership dues, endowment funds, contributions and grants from federal agencies, including the U.S. Department of the Interior, under provisions of the National Historic Preservation Act of 1966. Membership in the National Trust is open to all interested individuals, organizations, corporations and libraries. For information about membership and other National Trust programs, write to the address above.

Printed in the United States of America
96 95 94   7 6 5 4

Library of Congress Cataloging in Publication Data

Munro, Roxie.
   Architects make zigzags.

   Bibliography: p.
   Summary: An alphabet book of twenty-six architectural concepts, with drawings and definitions of such terms as dormer, facade, and newel post.
   1. Architecture—Dictionaries, Juvenile. [1. Architecture—Dictionaries] I. Maddex, Diane. II. Title.
NA31.M86 1986 720′.3 86-9479
ISBN 0-89133-121-2

Designed by Karren Leas, Design Solution, Ltd., Chevy Chase, Md.

Developed and edited by Diane Maddex, Editor, The Preservation Press, with Gretchen Smith, Associate Editor.

Composed in Goudy Old Style by Carver Photocomposition, Inc., Arlington, Va.

Cover: P is for Preservation. Drawing by Roxie Munro

Preface

I have always been fascinated by architecture; it provides all sorts of rich material for artists. To me, buildings are like huge sculptures, with interesting shapes and varied masses. Even the space created between buildings excites me. Most buildings seem very individual, like a person with his or her own character. Each one is made for a specific reason, by an individual architect or builder, at a particular time in history, and this makes each seem especially human.

The decorative elements in architecture are continuously amusing to me. Regardless of the function of a building, from the most magnificent to the most humble, humans manage to decorate their structures. All sorts of styles and patterns appear on buildings. It seems as though people feel a real necessity to go beyond function and to manipulate form. The ways in which this is done charm me immensely.

Roxie Munro
New York City

Introduction

This is a little book about a subject that is so big most people seldom stop to think about it. It's about architecture—all the buildings that surround us and shelter us as we live and work, go to school and play. There are many ways to begin to enjoy and understand architecture: Books and classes detail how buildings are built, what styles they are, who their architects were, what happened in them. But one of the best ways to start is just to *look* at architecture. Look up, to see what type of roof covers a house. Look down, to find an unusual fence in a yard. Look inside, to locate styles of windows. Look around, to pick out fancy ornament on a building—even zigzags.

But, best of all, have fun looking at architecture. Expand this alphabet with new words and places on your own street. And, once you start to enjoy architecture, think about ways in which you can help save the most enjoyable examples.

Architect

Architects make zigzags—when they want to really dress up a building—but basically what architects do is design and supervise construction of buildings and even whole towns. The name "architect" comes from the Greek word for master builder, but architects are not builders. They are form givers, transforming ideas and space into brick and stone and other materials.

An architect in his studio

Bracket

Brackets look like shoulders propping up projecting parts of buildings from roofs to porches and balconies. They appear to be very useful, but brackets often are built more for show than for function.

Honolulu House
Marshall, Mich.

Column

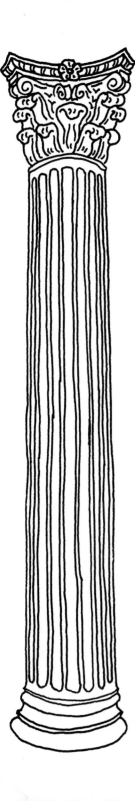

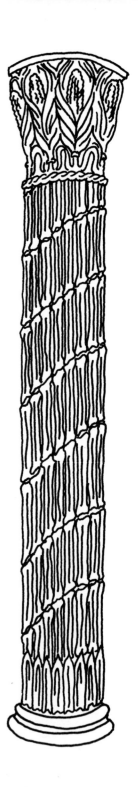

Columns hold up building sections like tall, thin legs. Most have a base (bottom), a shaft (middle section) and a capital (top) and are made of stone, concrete, brick, cast iron, steel, wood or similar strong materials. (Some columns look like stone but are really made of cast iron.) Different styles of architecture have their own special styles of columns.

Corinthian, Corncob, Tuscan, Egyptian and Ionic Columns

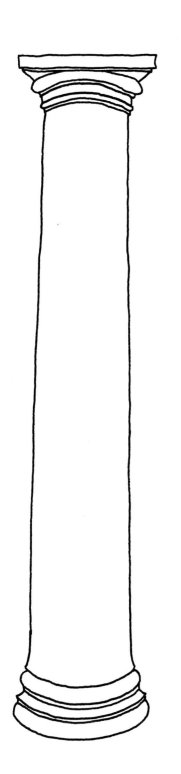
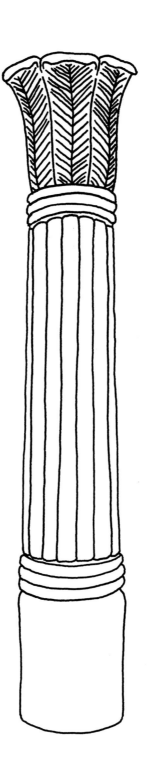
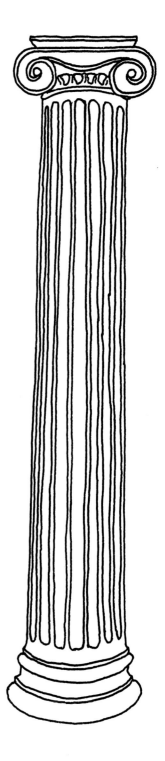

Dormer

Dormers are little windows that project like eyebrows from sloping roofs. They provide extra light and air and keep a plain roof from being boring. Some architects don't stop at one or two dormers; they like to sprinkle around dozens of them to make a building seem always surprised—and surprising.

Hotel Del Coronado
Coronado, Calif.

Eaves

Eaves are the shadowy undersides of overhanging roofs beginning where the roof meets the building wall. Eaves sometimes may be for the birds (to nest in), but they are also for people to take shelter under in rain and shine and to enjoy the dramatic angles they create.

Robie House
Chicago, Ill.

Facade

Facades are the faces of buildings. Because they are out front, they are usually the fanciest side of a building and contain the front door. There are almost as many types and styles of building facades as there are human faces, and most of them have eyes (windows) and a mouth (a door).

Haughwout Building
New York, N.Y.

Gable

Gables are triangles pointing to the sky from the walls of buildings that have high, pitched roofs. Houses with gables usually have two; some have four. This house with seven gables (two at the back) is unusual but famous.

House of Seven Gables
Salem, Mass.

House

Houses are buildings built especially for people to live, eat and sleep in. They are big and small, plain and fancy. Some houses are attached to make row houses; others are stacked atop each other to make apartment houses. In the city or in the country, houses are homes for us all.

Four-Square, Row House, Farmhouse,
Bungalow and Queen Anne Houses

Ironwork

Ironwork is visual delight masquerading as security. It is used for fences, balcony railings, gates and sidewalk grates, window and door hinges and other architectural details. Cast or wrought iron is molded or worked into often elaborate floral and geometrical designs — sometimes even cornstalks.

Short-Moran House
New Orleans, La.

Jigsaw Work

The Pink House
Cape May, N.J.

Jigsaw work is wood cut into scrolls and spirals and snaky patterns by power saws that make sharp and twisting curves. The invention of jigsaws in the 19th century started a rush to build wooden curlicues along roof eaves, porches and balconies. Jigsaw work is seldom made anymore, so you have to look at old buildings to find it.

Keystone

**K**eystones are wedge-shaped pieces of masonry (brick or stone) set in the center of arches. These stones are key because they are needed to lock an arch into place. A face or a construction date may be carved there, or a keystone may sport a symbol with a special meaning for its own building.

Truck Company No. 4 Firehouse
Washington, D.C.

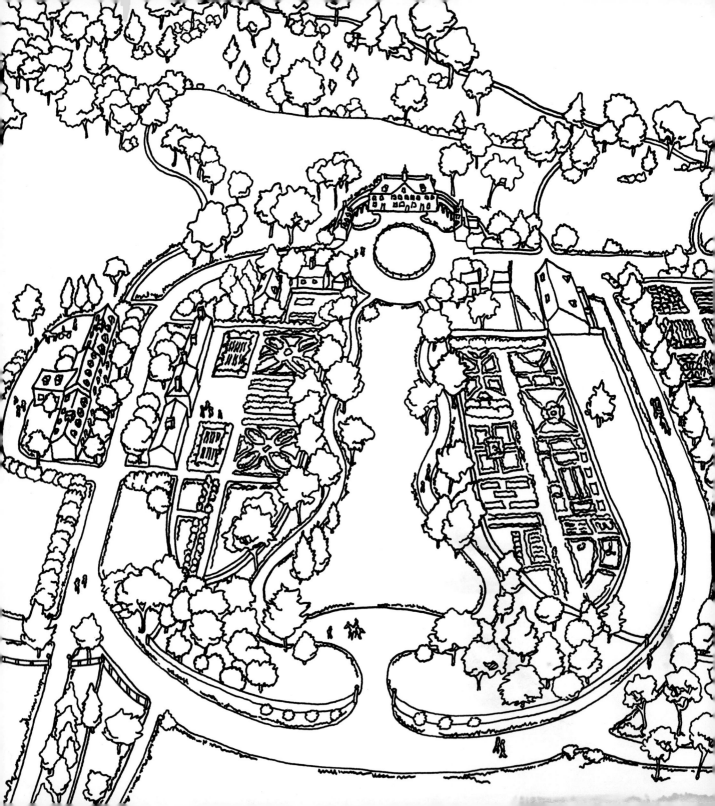

Landscaping

Landscaping is nature brought up to the edges of a building. It is trees, flowers, shrubs, pathways and ponds — everything that is done to shape the earth into a garden.

Marquee

Marquees are double-duty canopies found most often over entrances to movie theaters. They protect people waiting outside, but an equally important part of their role is to advertise the show and the stars to be seen in the picture paradise inside.

Paradise Theatre
Chicago, Ill.

Newel Post

ewel posts show where a stairway starts or stops. They are easy to spot because they anchor the banister and are usually bigger and fancier than the other stair rails. Newel posts are capped off with a resting place for a hand — a knob known as a finial that may be rounded or may even look like a pointed onion.

U.S. Custom House
Galveston, Tex.

Ornament

Ornament is anything an architect or builder wants to put on or in a building to make it fun to look at. Carvings, railings and paint are ornament, and so are roofs and doors and the textures of building materials. Ornament can be applied or built in, and almost every building has it.

White Elephant Saloon
Fredericksburg, Tex.

Preservation

Preservation is everything people do to keep buildings in working order and save them to be used another day. Making sure that the roof is watertight and the outside is painted helps preserve a house. So does joining a group to stop a landmark from being torn down. Preservation means caring for buildings worth saving.

Carson House
Eureka, Calif.

Quoin

Quoins sound a little like corners, and that is what they are: large or conspicuous stones set into the corners of outside walls. They help reinforce the edge as well as provide another way to make a building more interesting.

Cobblestone School
Childs, N.Y.

Roof

*R*oofs are the tops of buildings. They protect everything below from rain and snow, wind and weather of all kinds.
Roofs come in a variety of shapes and materials and can be used to make a building just as distinguished as a person wearing a hat.

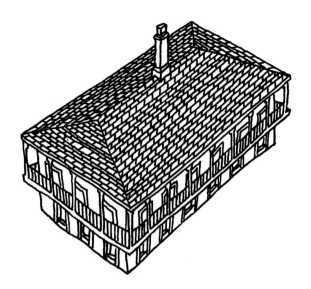

*Gabled, Gambrel, Hipped
and Mansard Roofs*

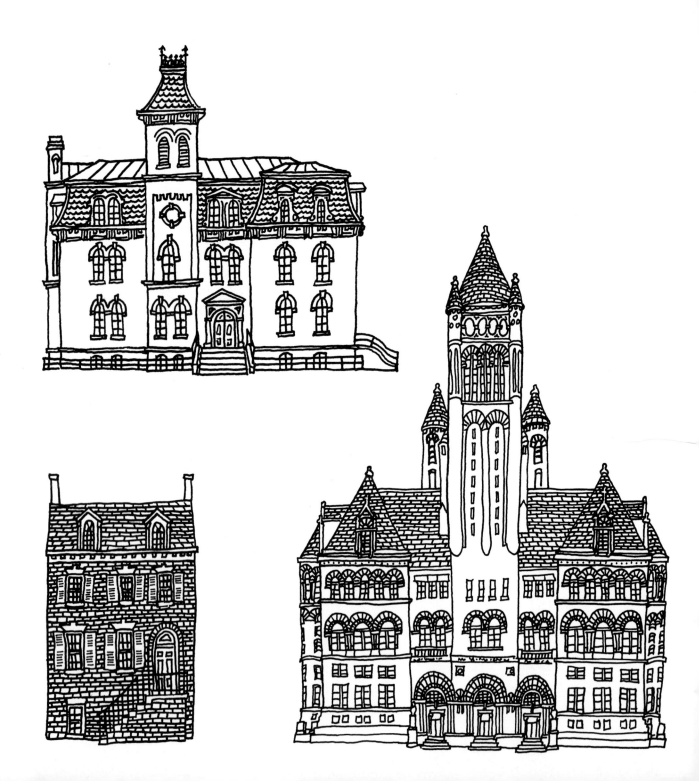

Style

Style is the way a building looks. It is form, not function. Throughout history, different styles of architecture have been popular at different times. Each style has its own way of arranging building parts and using ornament. All buildings may not be a formal style, but they all have some style.

Second Empire, Federal, Richardsonian Romanesque, Greek Revival, Gothic Revival and Italianate Styles

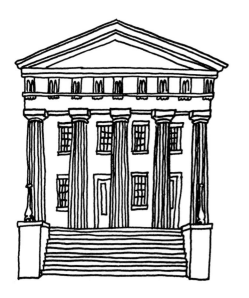

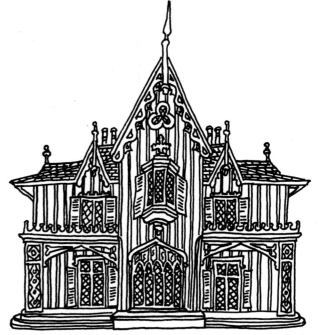

Tower

Towers are buildings or parts of buildings that are especially tall. They rise high above lower stories and the town below. Towers once provided secret places from which to watch people, but now towers are built mainly to call attention to themselves.

Jefferson Market Courthouse
New York, N.Y.

Utility

Utilities are the services we use every day from electricity and gas to water. They come to us in pipes and transmission lines from special utility buildings. Some people think these structures are ugly, but other people think they are fun—particularly when they are no longer used and are turned into a playground.

Gas Works Park
Seattle, Wash.

Veranda

Verandas are really just porches with a ritzier name. A veranda has a roof, a railing, tall posts, a floor and probably lots of decoration. It may stretch across the front of a house and makes a good place to sit and visit and watch the neighbors go by.

Victorian Veranda
Boalsburg, Pa.

Window

W indows are the eyes of a building that look out into the world and let others look in. They are built to let light and air into what otherwise would be a dark wall. Windows almost always have glass for protection from the weather and come in too many shapes and sizes to count.

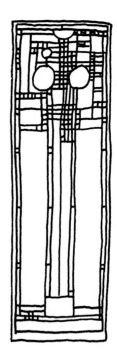

Italianate, Palladian, Gothic,
Leaded Glass, Bull's-eye,
Fanlight and Six-over-Six Windows

X Ray

X rays are pictures taken to see inside building parts just as they are used to see inside people. When a building is about to be restored, x-ray machines can photograph walls and wood to show pieces inside that are hidden to the eye—allowing builders to see what is there and what condition it is in without tearing apart the building to find it.

X-ray picture of an old stairway

Yard

$\mathcal{Y}$ards are enclosed or defined spaces around buildings. They can be set apart by a fence, hedge, wall, sidewalk or street and can contain as little as dirt or grass or as much as trees, plantings, benches, play equipment, tool sheds, a bird bath, a fountain, walkways or just about anything anyone wants to put there.

A yard with typical
19th-century furnishings

Zigzag

Zigzags are strings of M's, W's or Z's that zig and zag together like a chorus line around a building. The zigzag pattern has been used as decoration for many centuries, but it reached its peak of perfection in Art Deco buildings — and these are good places to look for in order to see why architects make zigzags.

General Electric Building
New York, N.Y.

The Illustrations

Architect. An architect at the drafting table in his studio.

Bracket. Honolulu House (Abner Pratt House), Marshall, Mich. Built: 1860.

Column. *Corinthian:* Oatlands, Leesburg, Va. Builder: George Carter. Built: 1800. *Corncob:* U.S. Capitol, Washington, D.C. Architect: Benjamin H. Latrobe. Built: 1809. *Tuscan* (with Doric capital): Tudor Place, Washington, D.C. Architect: William Thornton. Built: 1805–16. *Egyptian:* Medical College of Virginia, Richmond, Va. Architect: T. S. Stewart. Built: 1844. *Ionic:* Charles Q. Clapp House, Portland, Maine. Builder: Charles Q. Clapp. Built: 1833.

Dormer. Hotel Del Coronado, Coronado, Calif. Architects: James and Merritt Reid. Built: 1887–90.

Eaves. Frederick C. Robie House, Chicago, Ill. Architect: Frank Lloyd Wright. Built: 1907–09.

Facade. Haughwout Building, New York, N.Y. Architect: John P. Gaynor. Built: 1856.

Gable. House of Seven Gables, Salem, Mass. Builder: John Turner. Built: 1668.

House. *Four-Square:* The Langston. Builder: Sears, Roebuck and Company. Built: 1916–22. *Row House:* William Renshart Row Houses, Savannah, Ga. Built: 1852. *Farmhouse:* Belmont, N.Y. Built: about 1900. *Bungalow:* Hanchett Residence Park, San Jose, Calif. Built: about 1910. *Queen Anne:* 809–11 Pierce Street, San Francisco, Calif. Architect: A. J. Barnett. Built: about 1894.

Ironwork. Short-Moran House (Col. Robert Henry Short House), New Orleans, La. Architect: Wood and Perot. Built: 1859.

Jigsaw Work. The Pink House (Eldridge Johnson House), Cape May, N.J. Builders: Johnson Brothers. Built: 1882.

Keystone. Truck Company No. 4 Firehouse, Washington, D.C. Built: 1896.

Landscaping. Mount Vernon (George Washington's estate), Mount Vernon, Va. Builder: Augustine Washington. Built: 1743.

Marquee. Paradise Theatre, Chicago, Ill. Architect: John Eberson. Built: 1928. Demolished.

Newel Post. U.S. Custom House, Galveston, Tex. Architects: Cluskey and Moore. Built: 1861–65.

Ornament. White Elephant Saloon, Fredericksburg, Tex. Built: 1888.

Preservation. William Carson House, Eureka, Calif. Architects: Samuel and Joseph C. Newsom. Built: 1884–86.

Quoin. Cobblestone School (District 5 Schoolhouse), Childs, N.Y. Built: 1849.

Roof. *Gabled:* House in Maryland. Built: about 1860. *Gambrel:* Barn in Arkansas. *Hipped:* Casa Amesti, Monterey, Calif. Built: about 1834–46. *Mansard:* John De Koven House, Chicago, Ill. Built: 1874.

Style. *Second Empire:* McKinley High School, Lincoln, Neb. Built: 1872. *Federal:* House in Georgetown, Washington, D.C. Built: about 1820. *Richardsonian Romanesque:* Allegheny County Courthouse, Pittsburgh, Pa. Architect: Henry Hobson Richardson. Built: 1884–88. *Greek Revival:* Old State Bank, Shawneetown, Ill. Built: 1840. *Gothic Revival:* Roseland (Bowen House), Woodstock, Conn. Built: 1846. *Italianate:* Morse-Libby House, Portland, Maine. Architect: Henry Austin. Built: 1859–63.

Tower. Jefferson Market Courthouse (New York Public Library), New York, N.Y. Architect: Frederick C. Withers. Built: 1877.

Utility. Gas Works Park (formerly Washington Gas Company), Seattle, Wash. Built: 1906. Restoration Architect: Richard Haag Associates.

Veranda. Victorian Veranda, Boalsburg, Pa.

Window. *Italianate:* 1493–99 McAllister Street, San Francisco, Calif. *Palladian:* Mount Pleasant, Philadelphia, Pa. Built: 1761. *Gothic:* David McCully House, Salem, Ore. Built: 1865. *Leaded Glass:* Avery Coonley Playhouse, Riverside, Ill. Architect: Frank Lloyd Wright. Built: 1912. *Bull's-eye:* One Walnut Street, Boston, Mass. *Fanlight:* One Spring Street, Newburyport, Mass. *Six-over-Six:* Federal-style house in Princeton, N.J. Built: about 1785.

X Ray. X-ray picture showing the nails used to attach an old banister to the stair rails.

Yard. A yard with typical 19th-century furnishings.

Zigzag. Lobby, General Electric Building, New York, N.Y. Architects: Cross and Cross. Built: 1931.

Further Reading

Abramovitz, Anita. *People and Spaces: A View of History Through Architecture*. New York: Viking Press, 1979.

Devlin, Harry. *To Grandfather's House We Go: A Roadside Tour of American Homes*. 1967. Englewood Cliffs, N.J.: Four Winds Press, 1980.

———. *What Kind of a House Is That?* New York: Parents' Magazine Press, 1969.

Goldreich, Gloria and Esther. *What Can She Be? An Architect*. New York: Lothrop, Lee and Shepard, 1974.

Salvadori, Mario. *Building: From Caves to Skyscrapers*. Reprint. New York: Atheneum, 1985.

———. *Building: The Fight Against Gravity*. New York: Atheneum, 1979.

Tegland, Janet, ed. *Significant American Artists and Architects: A Picture and Text Reference*. Chicago: Children's Press, 1975.

Weitzman, David. *Underfoot: An Everyday Guide to Exploring the American Past*. New York: Scribner's, 1976.

Wilson, Forrest. *Structure: The Essence of Architecture*. New York: Van Nostrand Reinhold, 1971.

———. *What It Feels Like to Be a Building*. Washington, D.C.: Preservation Press, 1988.

The Illustrator

Roxie Munro is an artist whose work has been featured in several books and on covers of *The New Yorker*. Her books include *Color New York* (1985, Arbor House); *The Inside-Outside Book of New York City* (1985, Dodd, Mead), which was selected by the *New York Times* as one of the 10 best illustrated children's books of 1985; and *The Inside-Outside Book of Washington, D.C.* (1987, E. P. Dutton). Munro began her career as an editorial illustrator for newspapers and magazines and as a television courtroom artist. She received a B.F.A. from the University of Hawaii, attended Ohio University graduate school and studied painting at Yaddo. Her paintings and drawings have been shown at numerous galleries, including a one-person show at the Delaware Art Museum. Munro's work also is included in private, corporate and public collections. She grew up in the Chesapeake Bay area of Maryland and now lives in New York City.